THE
GREAT
GOLD TRAIN
ROBBERY

BUNCH OF
BADDIES

THE CACTUS BOYS

CAPTAIN MIDNIGHT AND
THE GRANNY BAG

GALACTACUS THE AWESOME

THE VOYAGE OF
THE PURPLE PRAWN

THE CHOCOLATE BUNNY PLOT

THE GREAT GOLD TRAIN ROBBERY

THE SMUGGLERS OF CRAB COVE

SUPER SPY, MISKIN SNYTHELY

THE GREAT GOLD TRAIN ROBBERY

Andrew Matthews

Illustrated by Guy Parker-Rees

ORCHARD BOOKS

for Jack
A.M.
for Ish (beware Nosher)
G.P.R.

ORCHARD BOOKS
96 Leonard Street, London EC2A 4RH
Orchard Books Australia
14 Mars Road, Lane Cove, NSW 2066
1 85213 910 2 (hardback)
1 86039 054 4 (paperback)
First published in Great Britain 1995
First paperback publication 1997
Text © Andrew Matthews 1995
Illustrations © Guy Parker-Rees 1995
The right of Andrew Matthews to be identified as the Author
and Guy Parker-Rees as the Illustrator of this Work
has been asserted by them in accordance with
the Copyright, Designs and Patents Act, 1988.
A CIP catalogue record for this book is available
from the British Library.
Printed in Great Britain.

CONTENTS

1. The Upstairs Room 7

2. Surprises 19

3. A Bunch of Yokels 34

4. Trussed and Foiled 45

WANTED

FOR SPITTING SWEARING AND
~ TRAIN ROBBERY ~

NOSHER NORRIS

JACK CARDEW

SHADY SAMUELS

HATTY HERRING

1

THE UPSTAIRS ROOM

There were many low-down riverside taverns in Victorian London, but the lowest down of them all was *The Grubby Griffin*. In fact, if it had been any lower down, it would have been under water. This shabby dive was the haunt of London's most desperate criminals. They gathered there to trade stolen goods, drink beer, spit and swear.

One warm summer's night, three such criminals met in the upstairs room of the tavern. They had each received a mysterious note.

The tallest person in the room was Nosher Norris. His shoulders were as broad as a doorway and his arms were so muscled, it looked as if he had snooker balls stuffed up his sleeves. Nosher was so strong that he could break open a brazil nut with his eyelids.

The shortest person in the room was Hatty Herring. Hatty had rosy cheeks and a sweet smile, but underneath she had a heart as tough as a dustman's boots. She was the best lock-picker and safe-breaker in the business and always wore kid gloves to protect her long, thin fingers. Hatty boasted that with just a piece of bent wire and an ear trumpet, she could open any lock in the land.

The most medium-sized person in the room was Shady Samuels. He had a square face and short grey hair that stood up on his head like iron fur. Shady was a master burglar. He had once burgled a house so quietly, he was able to steal the beds from under their sleeping occupants. When they woke in the morning, they found themselves lying on bare boards because Shady had taken the carpets as well.

The three villains knew each other well and they passed the time by telling stories. After the stories ran out, they played I-Spy and made rude noises until midnight chimed from a nearby church. A floorboard creaked and the thieves fell silent as the door of the room opened and

a man entered.

The man was holding a candle and its light shone on his slyly handsome face. His thin lips twisted into a smile. "Good evening, lady and gentlemen," he said in a voice that purred like a well-fed cat. "I'm so glad you were able to come."

" 'Oo are you, mister?" Hatty demanded suspiciously. "I ain't seen you before."

"Then let me introduce myself," said the stranger. "My name is Jack Cardew. I'm a cardsharp, cad and criminal mastermind."

"Is that right?" sneered Shady. "What d'you want with us, then?"

Don't 'e talk posh? D'you reckon I should duff 'im up lads?

"Why not wait until you've heard what I've got to say?" suggested Jack. "You're all experts and the top criminals in your fields...but how would you like to be even more? How would you like to be world famous and disgracefully rich?"

"Come off it, matey!" Shady snorted. "What are you– a music-hall comedian?"

"Far from it!" hissed Jack. "I'm deadly earnest!"

" 'Ang about," protested Nosher. "You said your name was Jack just now."

Jack Cardew ignored Nosher's interruption and carried on. "With you three to help me, I intend to carry out the most audaciously daring robbery in the whole history of crime."

"Oh, yeah?" Shady sneered. "What's that then– takin' bull's-eyes off a choirboy?"

"Or pinchin' the collection plate from Westminster Abbey?" suggested Hatty.

" 'Ow about swipin' some shrubbery from 'Yde Park?" Nosher sniggered.

The three criminals' mocking laughter flew around the room like a demented bat. Jack waited patiently for the laughter to die down, then said, "You underestimate me, lady and gentlemen. I'm planning a bank robbery."

"Is that all?" scoffed Hatty. "I've robbed loads! Why should a bank job make us all world famous?"

"Because the bank I'm talking about is the Bank of England," Jack said.

2

SURPRISES

Nosher was so astounded that he jumped in the air and bumped his head on the ceiling. Hatty's fingers curled and uncurled like startled woodlice calming down. Shady's hair lay down flatter than a cornfield after a thunderstorm. "The Bank of England?" they all said together.

"Yes, lady and gentlemen, the Bank of England!" Jack replied. "The ultimate challenge!"

"You're bonkers, mate!" declared Shady. "That place is locked up tighter than a tiger's cage."

"And it's swarmin' with armed guards," added Hatty.

"Yeah, and Swiss cheese," said Nosher.

"Swiss cheese?" Jack repeated with a frown.

"It's rhymin' slang, innit?" said Nosher. "Swiss cheese, police—geddit?"

"But Swiss cheese doesn't rhyme with police," Jack pointed out.

"Dunnit?" said Nosher. "I never could get the 'ang of this poetry lark."

Jack groaned quietly to himself, and then continued, "You're quite right!" Jack agreed. "To get into the vaults of the Bank of England would be an impossible task, even for master criminals like yourselves. That's why I propose to rob the bank without setting a single foot inside it."

Jack paused to reach into his coat and brought out a fat black book with a gold crest on the cover. "Do you know what this is?" he said.

"Yeah, a book!" said Nosher.

Not just any book. This is the Bank of England's secret train timetable.

"Where did you get that?" gasped Hatty.

"In a card game with a Bank of England cashier," Jack explained. "After I won it, he ran away to sea aboard a Swedish sloop." Jack flicked the book open with his thumb and when he spoke again his voice quivered with excitement. "According to this timetable, next Thursday at 11.30 p.m., a secret train will leave Southampton bound for London. My plan is to stop that train just outside Reading, overpower the crew and steal what it's carrying."

"And what's that?" asked Hatty.

Jack closed the timetable with a triumphant snap. "A million pounds' worth of gold bars," he said.

"A million pounds!" Nosher repeated hoarsely. "Why, if we split it four ways, we'd each get...er...lots!"

"'Old your row, Nosher!" said Hatty. She stared shrewd-eyed at Jack. "Come on, Mr Criminal Mastermind, 'ow many people are gonna be on that train? Fifty? An 'undred?"

"Three," said Jack. "The driver, the fireman, and the guard. They don't bother with anyone else because the train's so secret. That's the beauty of my plan!"

"Nah!" said Nosher. "The beautiful bit is where we all end up rich."

"Too right!" agreed Hatty. "It'd be nice to be rich. D'you know, I 'aven't been able to afford an 'oliday in years!"

"Me neither," said Shady. "I've always fancied foreign travel - you know, visitin' exotic places and pinchin' all their gear."

"All right, mister," Hatty said to Jack. "If you can convince us this plan of yours is any good, you can count us in."

"Splendid!" said Jack. "Now, because no one knows that we know about the secret train, we won't be expected. The most important thing is to take the train completely by surprise. That's why I have chosen Reading, because nothing exciting ever happens there."

"Oh, I get it!" Shady said. "We're goin' to take over a signal box, change the signals to red and then jump on the train when it stops, right?"

"No," said Jack. "But we are going to need some special equipment."

"What sort of special equipment?" asked Hatty.

"Three farmers' smocks, a milkmaid's outfit, a horse and cart and a cow," said Jack.

A day or two later, Renton Bladgett, who owned a farm near Reading, staggered into his cowshed carrying a bucket and a milking-stool. It was five o' clock in the morning and Farmer Bladgett wasn't fully awake yet. "Easy, Clover!" he said to his old Guernsey cow. "Don't you go kickin' over the bucket like you did yesterday!"

Farmer Bladgett yawned loudly, placed the bucket in Clover's stall, plonked down the milking-stool and plonked himself down on top of it. He was so sleepy that he spent several moments milking Clover before he noticed something was wrong.

The stall was empty.

Mrs Bladgett was in the kitchen kneading dough and she looked up in surprise as her husband burst in.

"What is it, Renton?" she said.

"Clover's been rustled!" panted Farmer Bladgett.

"You'd better 'itch old Dobbin to the cart and ride over to Constable Watt's 'ouse," said Mrs Bladgett.

"I can't," said Farmer Bladgett. "Dobbin and the cart 'ave gone as well!"

" 'Oo'd want to steal Clover and Dobbin and our old cart?" Mrs Bladgett asked, puzzled.

"And that's not all!" said Farmer Bladgett. "My smocks 'ave gone missin', and your milkin' dress, too! Mark my words, Betty, there's more to this than meets the eye!"

3

A BUNCH OF YOKELS

The following Thursday night, in a dark field not far from Reading, the train robbers made their final preparations. The railway line ran through the middle of the field, and the gang rattled up to it in Farmer Bladgett's cart, pulled by the faithful Dobbin. Clover was tied behind the cart, and as she ambled along she mooed continuously.

"What the devil's the matter with that animal!" snapped Jack Cardew. "She hasn't been quiet for the past hour!"

"She wants milkin', I expect," said Shady.

"Yeah!" Nosher said sympathetically. "Must be 'orrible 'avin' all them bottles rattlin' round your insides!"

"There's just milk inside the cow, Nosher," Shady explained patiently. "They put it in bottles after they get it out."

"Cor!" said Nosher. "What will they think of next?"

The cart stopped at the side of the railway line and the gang clambered down from it. Jack Cardew took a watch from the pocket of his smock and glanced at the luminous dial. "The train should be here in fifteen minutes," he said. "When it stops, Nosher will take care of the driver, fireman and guard while Shady and Hatty open the carriage. Then we'll load the gold bars on to the cart and make a clean getaway.

Is that all clear?"

"I suppose so," said Hatty. "But I don't 'alf feel a fool in this milkmaid's dress."

"At least your dress is clean. My smock smells of pigs," grumbled Shady.

"We look just like a bunch of farm 'ands!" Nosher complained.

"That's the whole idea!" Jack said
through gritted teeth. "If we all stood
round in masks and stripy jumpers, the
train driver would spot that something
funny was going on, wouldn't he? But if
he thinks we're local yokels, he won't
suspect us."

"Oh," said Nosher. "And 'ow did you say we were gonna stop the train? I didn't really get that bit."

"It's easy," Jack said with a sigh. "We stand the cow in the middle of the track and pretend that one of her hoofs is stuck. When the train comes along, we'll flag it down and ask for help."

"Oh, yeah!" said Nosher. "Piece of cake, innit? But, er, what if the train don't stop in time?"

"Then there'll be rather a lot of mince about the place," Jack replied. "Now let's get that cow on the line."

This proved easier said than done. Clover was in a bad mood. It was well past her usual milking time, she didn't like the look of the railway line, and when the gang tried to lead her on to it, she stubbornly refused to budge.

M-OO

Come on, nice cow!
Just stand on the line like a nice cow!
Here puss-puss.

"Right!" Jack said briskly. "This calls for a little brute force. Nosher, you push her from the back. Shady and Hatty will have to pull her from the front. I'll watch for the train."

"Huh! I notice you get the easy bit!" said Nosher, putting his shoulder to Clover's rump.

"I provide the brainpower," Jack
retorted. "Stop moaning and get a move
on. The train will be here any minute!"

It took a lot of heaving and yanking to
shift Clover, but eventually, with an
indignant "M-oo!" she clattered into the
gap between the railway lines, just as a
train whistle sounded in the distance.

"U-u-r!" cried Nosher. "Anyone got an 'anky? This cow's just done somethin' on my 'ead!"

"You'll have to leave it. The train's coming!" said Jack. "Get to your places and remember, if anything goes wrong, we use Plan B."

"What's Plan B?" Nosher enquired.

"We run like rabbits," Jack said grimly.

4

TRUSSED AND FOILED

There were lamps on the front of the engine of the secret train, and they lit up the track ahead. From time to time, the train driver glanced out of a little round window to check the line. When he saw a cow on the track, surrounded by a group of farm workers who were jumping up and down yelling, "Stop the train! Stop the train!", he pulled on the brake at once.

The train shuddered and began to slow. The wheels shrieked, spraying out more sparks than a Roman candle.

"What's up?" asked the fireman.

"See for yourself," said the driver.

The fireman popped his head out of the cab and saw for himself.

He found out soon enough, for when the train stopped, Jack Cardew stepped forward.

"You must help us, oo-ar!" he said, in a not-very-convincing rural accent.

At this point, the guard appeared. He had left his van at the rear of the train to find out what was causing the delay. "What's all this?" he demanded angrily.

"Oo-ar, your worship, we be a band of poor farm hands on our way to market, and our old cow has got her hoof stuck in the line," said Jack.

"Going to market–at this time of night?" said the guard.

"Ar! We like to get there good and early!" said Jack. "If you kind gentlemen would only help us, we can shift the cow and be on our way."

"I hope you realise that you're trespassing on railway property," said the guard. "That's a serious offence, liable to a fine of–" He stopped suddenly and frowned at Nosher. "What's that chap got on his head?" he asked curiously.

"A beret," said Jack. "They be all the rage round these parts."

"Oh, come on, let's give them a hand," said the driver. "We've lost enough time already. There'll be a terrible fuss if we're late with the you-know-what."

"All right then," the guard agreed grudgingly. "But I'm going to mention this in my report!"

The driver, fireman and guard hurried to the rescue of the unfortunate Clover, and ended up in need of rescue themselves. With a turn of speed surprising in someone of his size, Nosher overpowered all three and set about trussing them up tighter than a chicken at Sunday lunchtime.

Meanwhile, Jack, Hatty and Shady hurried to the rear of the train. The doors of the carriage containing the gold had been fastened with the finest and most up-to-date locks and bolts. They were made from solid steel, but it might have been toffee for all the difference it made. Hatty

and Shady had the doors open in no time. "Ea-sy! Ea-sy!" they chanted.

As the doors flew open, the robbers' faces were lit up by a golden glow. The gold bars were stacked neatly in the centre of the carriage floor, each bar about the size of a loaf of bread.

"I could stand here and look at it all night!" drooled Jack. "But there's work to be done. Form a line up to the cart. Hatty, hop in and start passing out those bars!"

Hatty climbed into the carriage, put her hands on a bar at the front of the pile and tugged. Nothing happened. Hatty strained until her face was red, but the bar stayed just where it was. "What are you playing at?" Jack

54

asked angrily.

"I can't lift it!" Hatty gasped. "It's too 'eavy, mate!"

"Nonsense!" Jack snorted. "Let me try."

A few moments later, Jack was as red-faced as Hatty and the gold bar was still in the same place.

"This stuff is far heavier than I thought!" Jack said. "Nosher, get in here and start hauling gold as quickly as you can."

It turned out that Nosher couldn't haul gold very quickly at all. He walked from the carriage to the cart, staggering under the bar's weight, and when he slammed it down on the back of the cart, there was a thump that made Dobbin

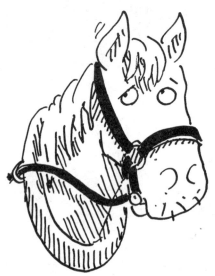

whinny. Jack, Shady and Hatty helped as best they could, but they could manage only a bar between two of them, with one taking a rest each trip.

With painful slowness, the load on the back of the cart grew larger and when, at last, the final bar was added to the pile, the whole cart began to creak like the hinges of a door in a haunted house.

The gold train robbers were so worn out that they could hardly pull themselves up on to the driving seat. Nosher fell asleep as soon as he sat down. Hatty and Shady fell asleep on either side of him, their heads slumped against his massive shoulders.

Jack Cardew picked up Dobbin's reins and flicked them. "Gee up!" he croaked wearily.

Dobbin whinnied and heaved with all his might, but once the cart was moving, it started to feel lighter with every step. In fact, it *was* growing lighter. One of the boards on the back had snapped under the weight of the load, and bar by bar the gold was dropping to the ground.

None of the gang noticed because they were all fast asleep—even Jack. In his dream Jack was driving the cart along the road to London, but Dobbin had actually taken a quite different direction. Clover joined her old friend, and the two animals walked side by side as they strolled along the winding lanes.

When the secret train failed to pass through Reading at the expected time, the station master alerted the local constabulary. A posse of stout-hearted policemen set out at once to locate the missing train. They found it, and the bound railwaymen.

The inspector in charge of the posse took only a few seconds to grasp the situation. "PC Tufnell, untie those railway employees!" he said smartly. "The rest of you men, follow that gold!"

The gold bars led all the way to Farmer Bladgett's barn, where the police found Jack, Hatty, Shady and Nosher in the cart, still asleep and snoring in chorus.

And so it was that the gold train robbers were foiled. The train driver, fireman and guard were given medals by Queen

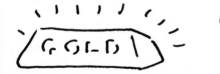

Victoria, and the policemen were all
promoted. Dobbin and Clover were given
special medallions to wear on ribbons
around their necks and Farmer Bladgett
was presented with a new cart by the
Governor of the Bank of England.

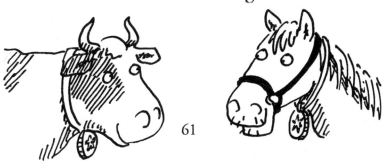

Jack, Shady, Hatty and Nosher were tried at the Old Bailey. Hatty was sent to Reading gaol and the rest were sentenced to hard labour at Dartmoor prison. They had plenty of time to repent of their criminal ways as they pounded rocks on the lonely moor in the cold drizzle of winter and the warm drizzle of summer.

They were all thoroughly miserable–except for Nosher. He must have learned something from the hours he spent with Clover, because when Christmas came he went to auditions and got the part of the cow in *Jack and the Beanstalk*, the Dartmoor Prison pantomime.

Nosher was the star of the show.

Here are another *Bunch of Baddies* for you to read…

CAPTAIN MIDNIGHT AND
THE GRANNY BAG
Stand and deliver! On Hangman's Heath the dastardly highwayman Captain Midnight lies in wait to rob the Royal Mail coach …but tonight he's in for a shock.

THE CACTUS BOYS
The toughest, meanest and fastest-shooting outlaws in the Old Wild West are the Cactus Boys …until they meet the sheriff of Lavender Gulch…

GALACTACUS THE AWESOME
Sam Brassworthy wasn't really expecting to be whisked on board an alien spaceship. But now it's up to him to save the Earth from the most terrifying monster from outer space.

THE VOYAGE OF THE PURPLE PRAWN
Hoist the sails and set course for Parrot Isle and buried treasure with blackhearted Abel Thinscratch and his pirate crew.